I'm in Love with a
BIG BLUE FROG

PERFORMED BY

Peter, Paul and Mary

WORDS AND MUSIC BY

Leslie Braunstein

ILLUSTRATED BY

Joshua S. Brunet

ICE C

imagine!
a Peter Yarrow Book

I'm in love with a
BIG BLUE FROG,
A big blue frog loves me.

It's not as bad as it appears,
He wears glasses and he's six foot three.

Well I'm not worried about our kids.
I know they'll turn out neat.

They'll be great lookin'
'cause they'll have my face,
great swimmers
'cause they'll have his feet!

Well I'm in love with a
BIG BLUE FROG,
A big blue frog loves me.

He's not as bad as he appears,
He's got rhythm and a PhD.

Well I know we can make things work.
He's got good family since,

His mother was a frog from Philadelphia,
His daddy an enchanted prince.

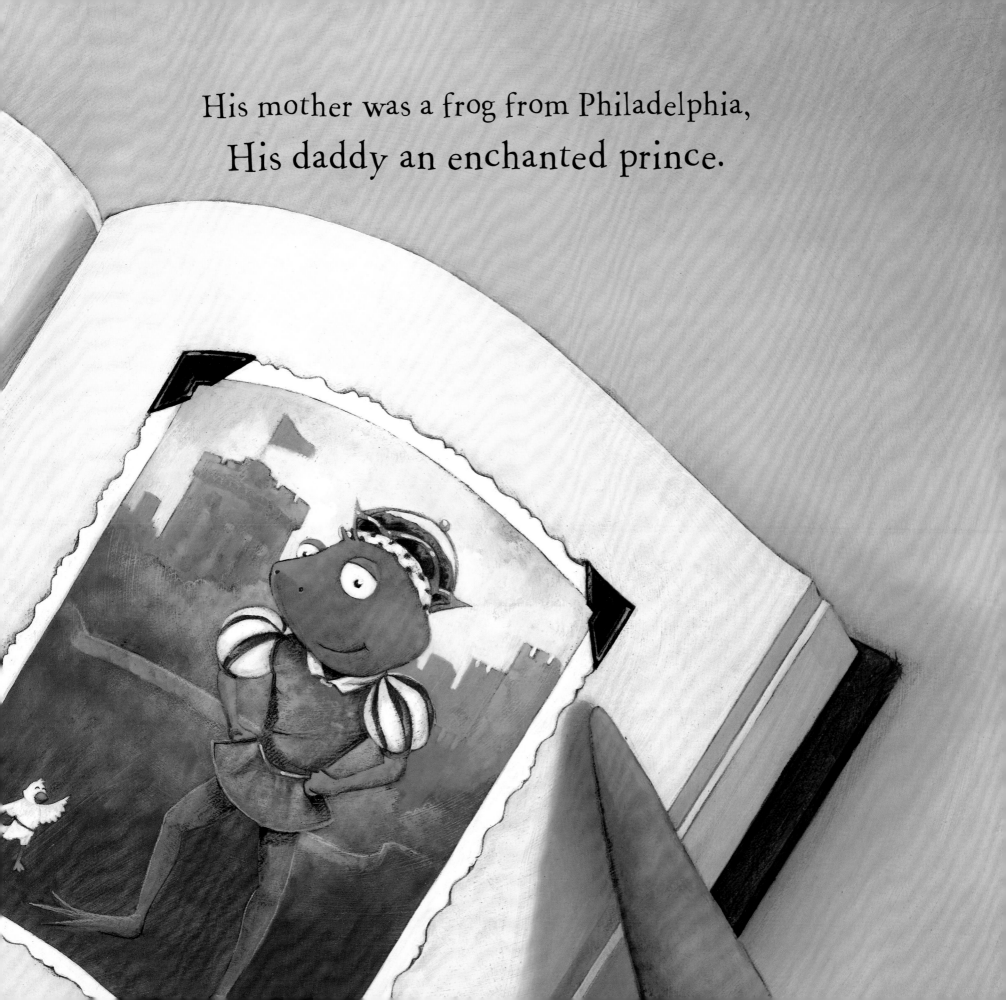

The neighbors are against it
and it's clear to me,
And it's prob'ly clear to you,

They think value on their property
will go right down
If the family next door is blue.

Well I'm in love with a
BIG BLUE FROG,
A big blue frog loves me.
I've got it tattooed on my chest,
It says **P.H.R.O.G.** (It's frog to me!)
P.H.R.O.G.

llustrator's Note:

What a blessing and a joy to have the opportunity to work alongside the legendary Peter, Paul and Mary. Their profound lyrics and exquisite melodies offered a tide of change that profoundly influenced the generations that were so influential to me. It's a great honor to now be a part of the impact and change their songs continue to call for as they reach a brand-new generation.

Performers' Note:

When Peter, Paul and Mary first heard Les Braunstein's "I'm in Love with a Big Blue Frog," we cracked up at the clever lyrics, the dry humor, and the song's charm, but we were also delighted to have found a song that treated an immensely important part of our lives in a less-than-serious way. The "big blue frog" clearly stood for African-Americans, and the girl who was in love with him symbolized our fellow Americans who were deeply committed to ending discrimination, segregation, and other painful remnants of slavery days. At the Civil Rights March on Washington in August, 1963, where Dr. Martin Luther King, Jr. delivered his historic "I Have a Dream" speech and, later, at the Selma–Montgomery March of 1965, we sang the inspiring yet still heartbreaking anthems "Blowing in the Wind" and "If I Had a Hammer." But in our concerts, we could also strengthen our resolve with laughter. Les had given us a wonderful new way to deliver our message, in a song that lit up the concert hall, with the audience singing and clapping along as an act of optimistic affirmation. With "Big Blue Frog," we could joyfully assert our belief that the struggle for equality before the law for all Americans would, one day, succeed.

Library of Congress Cataloging-in-Publication Data

Braunstein, Les.

I'm in love with a big blue frog / performed by Peter, Paul and Mary ; music & lyrics by Les Braunstein ; illustrated by Joshua S. Brunet.

p. cm.

Summary: A picture book version of a song made popular by the singing group Peter, Paul, and Mary

in which a girl proclaims her love for a 6'4"frog, whose mother is from Philadelphia and whose father an enchanted prince.

ISBN 978-1-936140-37-4

1. Folk songs, English--United States--Texts. [1. Folk songs. 2. Frogs--Songs and music.] I. Brunet, Joshua S., ill. II.

Peter, Paul, and Mary (Musical group) III. Title. IV. Title: I am in love with a big blue frog.

PZ8.3.B738Iak 2013

782.42--dc23

[E]

10 9 8 7 6 5 4 3 2 1

An Imagine Book

Published by Charlesbridge

85 Main Street

Watertown, MA 02472

617-926-0329

www.charlesbridge.com

Illustrated by Joshua S. Brunet

Performed by Peter, Paul and Mary

CD Copyrights and Details

Manufactured in China, September 2012.